DEDICATION

For my sons Toby and Tim and their gaming friends.

CONTENTS

ACKNOWLEDGMENTS

My first thanks go to the Year 6 Blue Group writers, who came up with the original idea for the beginning of the story, based on a picture from 'The Mysteries of Harris Burdick'. Thank you to all those who read the manuscript, making suggestions for improvements, and encouraging me to keep going – especially author Stephen Davies and my mother, Pauline Williams (who also coloured Amelia's pictures used on the book cover). Thanks to author Catherine Barbey for her helpful advice about publishing with Amazon. I would like to say a BIG thank you to my young editors who read the book with a critical eye and gave the thumbs up to publish: Corey, Matthew, Amaya, Emily and Alice - and to Myah, Bobby, Noah and Coralie for helping with the glossary words. Finally, a huge thank you to Amelia Gibson for agreeing to launch her illustrating career with such wonderful drawings that helped bring the characters to life.

I have added footnotes to help with more tricky words. If you learn a new word, do try to use it so it becomes part of your ever-expanding vocabulary bank.

REVIEWS

"The door to adventure, these thrilling chapters will keep you on the edge of your seat." Noah (8)

"I absolutely loved your book! It was incredible! I was hooked on the book when I was reading - there was tension all the way through the levels and it was action packed with adventures. All your ideas are totally original and extremely exciting: I have never read a book where someone goes into a game. I like the fact that you put all Toby's friends in the book too. The way I sum up this book is: it is amazing, and I would buy it if I saw it in the shops. Thank you for sending me your book. I really enjoyed reading it and I hope it gets published as I would definitely tell my friends about it." Corey (11)

"When I was reading the book, I felt like I was part of the story. It was amazing and I could picture every part of it in my head. Escape! is a great book and I really enjoyed reading it." Myah (9)

"A thoroughly enjoyable yarn." Paul (over 60 :)

1: THE DAY BEGINS

Toby woke slowly. He smiled as he realised it was the first morning of the long summer holidays. No school. No routine. No nagging. He stretched out his lanky limbs and listened: silence. Bliss. The empty summer's day stretched ahead. The only negative spoiling this carefree feeling was that Nick's old house, just a stone's throw away, stood empty. Since he had moved, way across town, they now relied on headphones to keep connected. "That's a point," he muttered, and swung his body round to switch on his computer...

The noise of the computer whirring into life and loading up Escape!, gave him away: moments later, Scamp was pawing at his leg. The dog's shiny, thick black curls were getting long, making it harder to see the warm,

chocolate-brown eyes looking up expectantly.

"OK. OK, you win," laughed Toby, as he bent down and ruffled the dog's head. After a final glance at the computer screen, he dressed quickly, grabbed his phone off the charger and went downstairs. The house was silent. He clipped on Scamp's lead, unlatched the back door and the two of them slipped out into the warm sunshine.

2: THE DOOR

Whistling, Toby sauntered[1] down the front path. Scamp happily trotted along beside him, eagerly sniffing the air for any new and exciting scents. The first tree proved irresistible and, forcing Toby to stop, Scamp investigated the grass around the tree's wide base with his sensitive nose. Whilst waiting, Toby pulled out his phone to quickly see who was up and wanting a chat. Pulling a face, he realised that the sun must have woken him before anyone else that summer's day since the screen remained unusually blank. Carefully

---

[1] sauntered – walking in a slow and relaxed way

replacing the device, he gave Scamp's lead a gentle tug to chivvy[2] him up.

On reaching the corner of Nick's old road, Toby felt drawn to make a short diversion to see the site of last summer's base. His group of friends had met there almost every day to play in the games room in the basement: a bank of computers, with huge screens, had completely occupied one end of the room. It was brilliant! They would play Escape! together as a team, even reaching the final level and finding the key on a couple of occasions.

Arriving at the familiar old house, Toby ran his fingers through his short fair hair as he stood gazing at the boarded-up windows, designed to keep out potential[3] mischief-makers; the lawn had become a meadow and bees buzzed around the purple lavender bush, as if calling Toby to come on in and join the fun. So, he pushed open the blue wooden gate

---

[2] chivvy – to try and make the dog hurry up
[3] potential – possibly might (cause trouble)

and strolled up to the front door - Scamp nervously followed him.

Expecting resistance, Toby stretched out his hand and turned the doorknob. The door was unlocked! He and Scamp looked at each other, wide-eyed. Scamp pawed at the door, which slowly opened – creaking – ominously[4] inviting them in.

"Well, this is a bit spooky, Scamp. What do you think? Should we have a quick look around for old time's sake?" Maybe it was a distant memory of the basement and the delicious snacks he'd eaten there, Toby didn't know - but something made Scamp dash inside. Dragging Toby behind, Scamp headed straight towards the small, wooden flight of stairs leading down to the gaming-room. Toby stopped abruptly where Scamp stood, ears pricked, at the top of the steps. Again, they looked at each other - a flicker of excitement glinting in Toby's playful green eyes.

---

[4] ominously – suggesting something bad may happen

They started down, haltingly[5], Toby clutching the bannister in one hand and Scamp's lead in the other. For once, Scamp wasn't pulling, so they descended slowly - gingerly[6] - stair by creaking stair. Toby was holding his breath with each step, hoping the wood was still solid - but also fearing, anticipating[7] what lay below. He had such happy memories of last summer – surely this place held nothing to fear?

On reaching the large basement, where before sat a bank of computers and a pool table, always surrounded by much laughter and chatter, he was greeted with silent emptiness. Nothing. Blank walls. Dusty wooden floor. All he could see in the half-light was an unusually small door in the wall facing him. Quizzically, he stared intently at it. Had that been there before? Scamp started to whimper - he glanced up with worried eyes at Toby and started tugging at the lead to go back – but no

---

[5] haltingly – stopping and starting, not feeling confident
[6] gingerly – carefully because he was afraid he might get hurt
[7] anticipating – expecting something

luck: Toby was now looking with interest at the low door - an impish grin playing around his mouth.

"I wonder what's behind that door, Scamp? It must have been covered up by computer screens when Nick lived here. Shall we have a quick look and then we'll carry on our walk? It's a bit creepy down here now that it's empty." They crept hesitantly to the door - Toby bent down and gripped the low handle. Taking a big breath to bolster his confidence, he turned the dull, brass doorknob and pushed open the door. He peered in. Complete darkness: not a hint of light anywhere... or was there? What was that green glow just

beyond his reach?

Ducking down, he almost crawled through the small space. Straightening up once more, he took a tentative[8] step towards the eerie glow, gripping Scamp's lead to keep him close by his side. Too late, he realised his mistake: with a sickening 'thunk!' the small door slammed shut.

---

[8] tentative – not sure it was what he wanted to do

3: THE OTHER SIDE OF THE DOOR

Wide-eyed in fear, Toby spun around, panic rising. He frantically scrabbled at where he thought the door was - but could feel no handles or doorknobs anywhere. All his clammy fingers could feel, was the outline of a large keyhole. A knot began to twist in Toby's stomach. What had they done? Hurriedly tugging his phone out of his pocket he flicked on the torch… His jaw dropped; his eyes grew wide; his mouth went dry. What!?

With the knot of fear growing in his stomach and the smile long gone from his face, he realised where he was... He knew *exactly* where he was. This was the door out of Escape! – the game they played last summer, here in this house: he recognised the flaky blue paint of the door, the ivy dangling down each side and there, on the left-hand side, was The Keyhole. All that he did *not* have was The Key.

Breathing fast, short breaths, his fear was now tinged[9] with a hint of excitement. He *knew* where The Key was… He knew *exactly* where The Key was. The trouble was, he knew what lay between The Key and himself. A tug in his hand made him look down: he'd completely forgotten that he had Scamp with him. Well, this was going to add a new dimension to Escape! – he had never played it with a dog in tow. He had completed the game last summer, and even a couple of times since then, so he knew he could do it; although, never before had his life depended on it – and not just *his* life – Scamp's too.

---

[9] tinged – with a little bit of something added to it

There was just one element missing from the usual format of the game – a team – his team — the best team! It was time to rally[10] the troops to help get him out of Escape! and back through the door to freedom. But before he could even get his phone back out of his pocket to call his friends, Scamp tugged so hard that Toby dropped the lead; the naughty little dog dashed off towards the green glow, barking his head off. "Scamp! Stop!" yelled Toby. Without delay, he followed him at full tilt[11]: he knew what was lurking[12] beyond the clearing in Level One.

Reaching the area of bright, lush grass, the source of the green glow, he wildly searched for Scamp, who had stopped barking and fallen ominously silent. Straining to hear the smallest sound, Toby frantically looked all around; even in the undergrowth beneath the huge trees guarding the clearing, there was not

---

[10] rally – bring his friends together to help him
[11] at full tilt – as fast as possible
[12] lurking – creeping around and maybe waiting to pounce

a sound. The naughty hound must have gone further. Toby needed his extra eyes – his team.

Stuffing an earbud in his ear with one hand, he punched Nick's number into his phone with the other and paced agitatedly[13] as he waited for a reply. "Come on! Come on!" he gasped, almost jumping up and down in impatience. A sleepy voice came through the earbud:

"What's the time? How come you're up already? Have you forgotten it's the holidays?"

"Nick! Nick! I need your help!" Toby blurted out excitedly, "You'll never believe what's happened – where I am. I'm in Escape!... I'm actually *in* Escape!"

"Can't we play later? Can't you let me sleep just a little more?" pleaded Nick.

"You don't understand - I'm not just playing the game, I'm *in* the game!" exclaimed Toby.

"What? How?" Nick asked - confused.

---

[13] agitatedly – excitedly and nervously at the same time

"I was passing your old house and the door was open, so I came in and went through a tiny door in the basement." Toby was waving his arms around as he spoke, going through the events that had brought him to this world of adventure.

"What tiny door? I don't remember a tiny door," Nick interrupted, annoyingly.

Toby continued impatiently, "Well it's there now... and I stupidly opened the door and decided to investigate a green glow coming from inside. The door shut behind me and I can't get out: there's no handle inside. But I know where I am – it's the door at the end of Escape!"

"No way!" exclaimed Nick, his mind spinning.

"It is! Honest! I need to get the key, but I need your help. Boot up and you'll see me on the screen," said Toby. "Oh, and by the way, there's a little black dog in the game now – Scamp!"

Toby heard the thump as Nick sprung out of bed to boot up his computer.

"Wicked! I see you!" enthused Nick, excitedly, "Don't worry – we'll get you out!" cried Nick. "What an adventure! I'm going to switch to my headphones while I get the rest of the gang to join the game. I'll get back to you," explained Nick.

Although it was unnerving[14], once more being totally alone, Toby was relieved that help was on the way. Turning his attention to locating Scamp, he set off along a path leading

---

[14] unnerving – making him feel worried and slightly afraid

out of the clearing and further into the game. With his team, he knew it was possible to get through all the levels, although it was always tricky. With a dog too, it was going to be almost impossible.

As he continued to search the forest, he wondered who Nick would be able to rouse at this time in the morning. Harry was an online friend – they'd been friends for years now, but they'd never met. A similar kind of friend was Biscuit – a newer recruit to the team but an asset, especially for killing off thieves in Level Three. Ryan was away, so he knew they would be at least one member down. That left Bailey – dependable, skillful Bailey. He would get him out of any scrape... so he hoped... oh how he hoped that Bailey was up!

Of course, the kingpin was Nick; to get the key in Level Four was Nick's specialty; crossing the river to reach the waterfall could be tricky, but Nick had an uncanny[15] knack of knowing where the stepping-stones were and

---

[15] uncanny – strange and difficult to explain

when they would appear. Relying on him to complete the quest was the only way they were ever going to get out of this game.

4: LEVEL ONE – THE DRAGON

Toby stood for a moment to take in the scene before him, constantly scanning the area for any signs of the little, curly, black dog. Tall trees, all hues of green and brown, were towering like skyscrapers from this unfamiliar vantage[16] point. On the computer, they had just seemed like any old trees, but from down here on ground level, they were enormous – like green giants. He felt like an ant – tiny - insignificant[17]. Thank goodness he wasn't alone in this quest.

---

[16] vantage point – a position from which you watch something
[17] insignificant – too small to be thought important

Beneath the dense trees was a tangle of undergrowth: vines, creeping up the trees, and bushes with brightly coloured flowers. Much of the detail was lost on the computer, but standing here, the colours and life-like flutter of leaves and grasses were incredibly real.

Just off to the right, the sparkling lake caught his eye – the game's destination: memories of last summer flooded back - the great feeling you got when your little boat glided to a stop and you were safe at last, with key in hand, to make your escape. Scents of the forest filled his nostrils, bringing him back to the present as he took in long breaths to bolster his courage and calm his nerves.

Level One was definitely one for a team. Hidden around the forest were chests, that concealed weapons which were necessary to defeat the dragon protecting the gate to Level Two. Toby knew where the shield chest was – selecting the finest one was always his contribution to the team's arsenal[18]. He would

---

[18] arsenal – a collection of weapons

have to trust that Nick could raise the rest of the gang and that they would get the other bits of armour – the helmet, sword and dagger, bow and arrows. As long as one member of the team defeated the dragon, they could all advance in the game. Once the dragon fell, they had a full sixty seconds to get through the gate – plenty of time.

Suddenly, the hairs on the back of his neck stood on end. A rustling in the undergrowth became a crashing and out from the trees appeared two avatars running straight at him. Instinctively, he crouched down low and put up his arms to protect himself from the inevitable[19] attack. The two figures launched themselves at him and he was flattened under a laughing heap of angular bodies.

"Toby! It's us!" shouted the two figures, hooting with laughter. Tears coursed down Toby's cheeks, but he wasn't embarrassed, just totally relieved to have their company. He

---

[19] inevitable – the attack was coming and he couldn't stop it

hadn't realised just how anxious he had been.

"You look so funny!" exclaimed Toby to Nick and Biscuit. "It's brilliant that you're here. Did you manage to get the others up Nick? Have you seen Scamp? I lost him at the beginning and can't see him anywhere."

"They're both on their way: Bailey and Harry," said Biscuit, "so we've a strong team."

"Ryan is away," explained Nick, "but hopefully we'll get through with just the 5 of us. We can do it!" However, a look of concern passed over Nick's face as he went on, "I think I saw Scamp, but he was running straight towards the dragon, so we'd better get a move on if he's any hope."

More crashing and snapping of twigs brought the final two boys hurtling[20] towards them. They welcomed them with open arms. "This is wicked!" shouted Harry "What a brilliant day this is going to be!"

"Hey guys! Brill! You do all look funny as avatars.... Do I look like me or like my avatar?" asked Toby quizzically, unable to see his friends' expressions because of their avatar form.

"You look like a blurry glitch! At least you're dressed like your avatar so it's easy to see who you are," Bailey said.

"Hey, this is crazy seeing you for the first time in a game, Toby," exclaimed Biscuit, Harry nodding in agreement beside him: whereas Nick and Bailey were school friends, Harry and Biscuit were both online-friends - together they formed Toby's head-phone community, that Mum always found such a weird idea. Biscuit reached out a squared arm

---

[20] hurtling – moving very fast

and tried to shake Toby's hand in greeting. They both fell about laughing.

Picking himself up off the floor, Biscuit, in his distinctive green top and yellow trousers, stood before the others. "Let's split up and get the weapons," he suggested, "and meet back at the well." A bright red structure, they used the well as a meeting place frequently when playing Escape! as it was easily visible through the trees. So, knowing exactly where they needed to get to, they agreed on the plan. It was nearer to the gate to Level Two than they were now, but far enough away from the dragon to give the chosen warrior time to get kitted out to fight. There was an added bonus to the well: it provided a chance to get a refreshment token, thereby increasing their power and ability to complete the game.

"One question before we go...." said Bailey, his bright blue and red stripy avatar standing out against the darkness of the forest around them, "Who's going to fight the dragon?"

"Toby, of course!" Harry exclaimed,

"Who'd miss a chance like this? To really fight the dragon as a real person, not with these rigid limbs." He laughed, his long yellow hair bouncing up and down as he jumped around to demonstrate the unbending avatar limbs the boys all had – apart from Toby of course – he was real – this was going to be a real fight.

Toby, feeling everyone's eyes on him, took some deep breaths and bit his lip as he thought about what lay ahead. Did he really want to fight the dragon? He didn't want to look like a chicken in front of the others, but he had a bit more at stake than them – they could just come back again for the next game – failure for him would be a bit more final!

Trying to look braver than he felt, Toby smiled weakly and slowly nodded his head. "I guess you're right, but make sure you find the best weapons!" With a worried look, he added, "And keep looking for Scamp – I don't know what I'd do if I had to leave him behind."

With that, they all hurtled off in

different directions, towards the chests to obtain weapons and armour: the toughest helmet, the sharpest sword and dagger, the most-deadly arrows with a strong, flexible bow. As for himself, Toby would make sure he got the shield that gave the best protection but wasn't so heavy that he couldn't actually fight. He *had* to win. He *had* to get home. He *had* to find Scamp. His forehead creased in a frown - the naughty, inquisitive, friendly dog – where could he be? He was probably searching out treats in this place that was full of new and interesting scents. Or worse still, he might try and make friends with the dragon!

Toby set off along the right-hand path that he knew led to the chest of shields. The path was soft with fallen pine needles underfoot, making his tread silent. He ran with an easy, regular stride – his long legs enjoying the exercise. He laughed wryly[21] as he realised this was the first time that he had felt tired in Level One: avatars didn't feel

---

[21] wryly – thinking it was funny but also a bit disappointing

anything – pain, tiredness, happiness - nothing.

Looking up, he realised he had come further than he thought and was nearly there. Cutting into the undergrowth to his right he soon spied the chest; it stood at the foot of the tree with the gnarly[22], double trunk and peculiar lime-green, shield-like leaves with their bright purple spines.

Before heaving up the heavy, wooden lid, he stood a moment to catch his breath, searching all around for any signs of Scamp. Was that a distant bark he heard in the quietness around him? He listened intently for a couple of seconds before shaking his head. Turning back to the chest, he grasped the handle and hauled the chest-lid open until it stood upright at a right-angle. Reaching down into the chest, he searched out the shield he knew he wanted for this all- important battle – the one he *had* to win. Catching sight of his favourite shield, he grasped it tightly and heaved it out. It was royal blue with a brass

---

[22] gnarly – twisted and rough

boss on the front and an arm support to both carry the weight and also help him to angle it against the dragon's slashing teeth and claws. Shield in hand, Toby headed back to the path that would lead him to the next step in his quest.

5 THE BATTLE

A few moments were all that was needed to reach the place on the path where you first caught a glimpse of the bright red well. His heart started pounding in his chest. He realised he was breathing faster again. Sweat began to prickle the back of his neck. Could he do this? He *had* to. He would.

As he approached the well, he heard his friends chatting to each other online: "Do you think we should each take a challenge and protect Toby?" suggested Nick.
"Naah... I think he wants to face the dragon," said Harry. "I know I would," he

continued, a little arrogantly[23].

"But I think Nick's right," Bailey insisted, "what if he doesn't make it? How will Scamp get home?"

"I think that would be the least of his worries!" laughed Nick, whose avatar was dressed in red and white stripy top and black trousers.

"Maybe you guys are right," agreed Biscuit, "If we take turns to face the dangerous challenges in the game, we can protect him. All he needs to do is arrive at the waterfall in Level Four with Scamp and get himself home."

"OK, OK," agreed Harry reluctantly. "But in that case, it's *my* turn to face the old dragon then," he blurted out, gallantly[24]. The dragon was fierce, so it took courage to face him alone, even with good weapons and armour.

Toby arrived at the clearing, already breathing more easily now he knew their plan.

---

[23] arrogantly – proudly, but in not a very nice way
[24] gallantly - bravely

At least he had agreed initially, so there was no shame. He looked around at his friends – their serious faces, bright coloured bodies and cuboid black feet, all clutching a piece of armour, each one the best of its kind, to give the greatest chance of success. They had all had a refreshment token and were back up to full strength.

"I overheard you all talking," admitted Toby. "Although I would have fought the dragon, I think you're right. I *must* get Scamp home or Mum will never forgive me. So, thanks guys." He looked around the circle of friends and nodded his thanks.

"Well let's see what we've got then," suggested Nick, bringing them all back to the challenge ahead. His dark brown hair was in a spiky style like Toby's - but unlike Toby's, Nick's avatar hair needed no gel to keep it spiked.

The players all threw down their weapons and Harry got kitted out[25]. The shiny

---

[25] kitted out – put on the equipment he needed to fight

helmet and shield would give good protection; the heavy sword and razor-sharp dagger would kill the dragon. Under cover of the trees, Bailey, the master archer, would swiftly fire arrows at the dragon to help Harry win the battle. Each arrow that struck the dragon would increase Harry's strength and give him more chance of winning.

Standing dressed as a warrior, with the dagger clipped into his belt, Harry swished the sword around to get the feel of it and did a couple of pirouettes[26] as if to limber up. "Right guys – let's go for it – got your bow and arrows, Bailey?" he queried.

"I'm ready – give me a moment to sneak up and get in position," whispered Bailey, as he slunk off into the undergrowth in the direction of the gate and its lethal green guardian.

Harry confidently saluted the others and then turned, braced himself and charged

---

[26] pirouettes – twirls like a ballet dancer

towards his waiting adversary[27], sword draw and raised. The others followed at a safe distance, all taking positions behind the trees that stood like sentries at the edge of the grassy battle arena in front of the gate.

In the centre of the bright yellow clearing was an even brighter green dragon, fire snorting out of flaring nostrils and claws slashing like daggers at Harry, who had charged towards him, sword swirling - fearless, fun-loving, brave Harry – giving his all for the team.

---

[27] adversary – his opponent in the fight: the dragon

Suddenly, the dragon flinched as a tiny arrow pierced his arm. He knocked it off and continued to slash mercilessly at the small figure below him. Bailey, the dependable sharp-shooter, kept up a stream of annoying arrows – none would kill the dragon, but they would distract him and weaken him and moreover, give Harry extra strength to make the kill. Harry gave out a great howl as the dragon's swipe found its mark. He fell to the ground, wounded, his pale blue top turning a shade of red, showing that his game-life was ebbing[28] away. Toby and the boys groaned with disappointment as they watched their chance of getting to Level Two also begin to ebb away.

Groaning, however, soon changed to cheering as, with a final surge of strength, gained from Bailey's arrows striking the scaley dragon, Harry pulled himself up. He discarded the heavy sword and lunged at the dragon's vulnerable[29] under-belly with the dagger, which

---

[28] ebbing – fading
[29] vulnerable – unprotected and at risk

he had snatched from his belt. It flashed as he drove it with all his might into the fleshy green middle. The dragon now roared - he too began to turn from green to red. With a final, fiery snort, the old dragon toppled down, pinioning[30] Harry's legs beneath the massive green body.

"Run guys! Quick! Through the gate!" urged Harry, selflessly, his voice faltering as his avatar increasingly turned red.

"Wait!" implored Toby, "I can't go without Scamp. Scamp! Scamp!" he yelled. After the noise of the battle, silence once more descended on the clearing. In the distance, an excited bark could be heard, getting nearer and nearer.

"Quick, Toby – go and find him," urged Nick, "We can see the timer counting down and you only have thirty seconds left before the door locks."

Toby dashed back across the clearing in

---

[30] pinioning – holding down his legs with the dragon's weight on top of them, so Harry couldn't move

the direction of the barking, calling for Scamp
to come. If only he was a more obedient dog!
At last, he caught sight of a little black shape,
racing towards him – ears flapping as he
bounded across the clearing.

Knowing that time was short, Toby
himself started running back towards the gate,
hoping Scamp would follow. From the
doorway, he turned back and saw Scamp had
stopped by the dragon, sniffing around this
unfamiliar creature.

"Come Scamp! Come!" he shouted,
beckoning wildly in frustration. Then he
resorted to the only command that brought the
dog to heel…. "Goodbye Scamp! Goodbye!"
and he turned, leaping through the door to join
the others, just as the sixty seconds was up and
it started to swing shut.

6: LEVEL TWO – THE GEMS

A split second before the gate clanged shut behind the four boys, a small, black, curly dog streaked through. "Scamp!" shouted

Toby, joyfully, grinning from ear to ear as he scooped up his pal and hugged him close. Scamp excitedly licked Toby's face and his fluffy tail wagged as if it would fall off. "Where have you been, little fella?" asked Toby.

"Woof. Woof," barked Scamp in a vain effort to reply.

"Well, that's one mystery solved!" remarked Biscuit, sarcastically. "I guess we are down to four now, which makes it a bit tricky, but we'll just have to do our best. Poor old Harry. You'll just have to watch and join in the next game, Harry."

They all stood and waved at the sky as if they could see Harry's human controller on his computer at home. "Thanks Harry!"

"Don't worry guys," he reassured them. "I'll watch to see if Toby makes it home this time! If not, I might just have to find the little door myself and rescue him that way."

"Well let's get cracking with finding the gems. It's a real pain they change their location each game. I suggest we split up and search," suggested Nick, taking charge. "Remember," he continued, "we need all five gem slots filled at the gate – so someone will have to find two. Plus, of course, we have the timer again – just sixty seconds after we find all five gems to get them into the right boxes at the gate, so no hanging around."

They all agreed to the plan and headed off in different directions. Toby bent down to pick up Scamp's lead, but it was gone. "I wonder how you lost that, Scamp?" he asked. Trusting brown eyes gazed up at him, offering devotion[31] but no explanation. "Well just stay close and help me sniff out some gems." At the word 'sniff' Scamp's ears pricked up and he started sniffing the air in every direction to see where Toby had hidden the treats. "No, no Scamp – no treats here. But let's see if your sensitive nose can find me some gems!"

Around them was a fairly boring, brown and green landscape, with grey rocky hills, small stands of trees, all shades of green, and

---

[31] devotion – love and loyalty for a person

shallow pools of twinkling, blue water. He could see Biscuit's bright green top and wavy blond hair in the far left of his vision as he searched amongst some rocks. Nick had headed for some trees to the right and Bailey had set off for a flower-covered hill to the left of them. Toby and Scamp headed towards a more distant low, rocky hill, checking on the way in a couple of the brown wooden chests that were strewn around randomly. The only places he knew to be wary, were the areas of sand, some of which were quicksand, which could swallow you so fast you hardly had time to call out.

"Got one!" came Nick's voice, triumphantly. He came bounding out of the trees, clutching a large, round, shiny orb, bright red in colour. "This ruby was hidden in a fruit tree - pretending to be an apple!" he chuckled.

"I've got one too!" yelled Biscuit, scrabbling back down the rocks, also clutching a large gem. His was a sparkling sapphire, deep blue, like his eyes. He flicked his head with satisfaction, making his plastic-like golden hair swish slowly. "Nick, why don't we carry the gems to the blue well and leave them there while we look for the rest?"

"Good idea." nodded Nick. "Hey! Watch out for that sandy bit… we don't want to lose another person," he said to Biscuit, who had veered away from sinking-sand, just in time.

Meanwhile, Toby and Scamp were looking under every rock on a small hill; around the back of the mound, they discovered a cave. Scamp stood still and growled, ears pricked up and staring straight ahead into the dark, inky depths of the cave. Straining to see into the blackness, Toby squinted and whispered to Scamp, "What can you see? What can you smell?"

As Toby's eyes became accustomed to the dark, he could gradually make out some glowing lights, bright yellow and deep pink. What were they? He felt decidedly uneasy[32] and started to back away when, out of the corner of his eye, he noticed a sparkling green shape, larger than the other lights, in the darkness of the cave. A gem! There were never any extras, so he had little choice but to venture into the cave to retrieve it – the team's success in the game, along with his freedom, depended on it.

Just as he was about to take the first step, Biscuit came around the side of the hill and stopped beside Toby. "Goblins!" he said, hands on hips and nodding in recognition of the eyes staring out at them from the cave. "They protect the emerald," he added. "I

---

[32] decidedly uneasy – quite worried and uncomfortable

know because I have tried several times to get the emerald from this cave - each time the pesky goblins get me before I can get back out. It's one reason this level is hard to achieve," explained Biscuit.

"Got one!" came Bailey's voice from somewhere off to their right, making them jump as they stood silently considering their predicament[33]. Passing through to Level Three without the emerald was impossible, so they were going to have to do their best.

As an idea suddenly came to him, Toby grinned, his green eyes twinkling: "Cat!" he shouted excitedly at Scamp, stabbing his finger into the air as he pointed into the cave. Scamp jumped to attention and started looking all around for the non-existent cat; but that never stopped him in the garden at home from prancing around, barking his head off at the place where he thought the neighbour's huge, hairy grey cat had been. "Cat! Cat!" yelled Toby, jumping up and down and pointing

---

[33] predicament – difficult situation

wildly in the direction of the glowing eyes. Scamp's legs were unbending as he gamboled around like a spring-lamb, just inside the cave, barking excitedly at anything that moved, protecting his master from the nasty 'cat'.

Toby's eyes shone with glee and relief when he saw the glowing eyes of the goblin-guardians fading into the depths of the cave - retreating from this barking menace. Seeing his chance, Biscuit bravely darted forward and grabbed the glowing green emerald. As he turned to exit the cave, leathery green arms reached out for his legs to make him fall. He faltered[34], stumbling as their creepy fingers almost found their mark. But he was nimble and sidestepped the sweeping arms and grasping fingers.

Whooping with delight, Biscuit raced into the daylight of Level Two clutching the prize: a sparkling, deep-green emerald. The boys laughed together as they ran towards the blue well. Nick was there with Bailey, who had

---

[34] faltered – moved unsteadily, unsure about going on

cleverly discovered the purple amethyst amongst the colourful flowers on the hill. When they heard how Scamp had helped Biscuit to snatch the emerald, they bent down and patted the curly black dog, who delightedly rolled over for a tummy rub.

Now they had four gems: the red ruby, the blue sapphire, the purple amethyst and finally the green emerald. That still left the diamond. "OK guys. Anybody got any clues where the diamond might be?" asked Nick, looking round at his teammates.

"Nope," said Biscuit, "but after all that running I think I need my refreshment token to get a bit more energy."

By this time, Toby himself was feeling quite parched and Scamp had his tongue hanging out for a drink too. So, Toby decided to try and let the well bucket down to get some actual water. A refreshment token, which revived your avatar on the computer screen, was not going to give him and Scamp any refreshment at all. He had no idea if the water was real and would do the trick, but it was worth a try.

He strode over to the handle by the well and, despite its protesting squeals, managed to crank it a turn. He peered over the brick wall around the well to see if it had had any effect. To his relief, he saw that the blue bucket had indeed descended a fraction. The well was dark inside, so he didn't know how far down the water was. He continued to rotate the handle until he heard a welcome splash as the bucket hit the water, far below. "Yeah!" shouted Toby excitedly. "That sounded like real water, Scamp. I think we are going to get a drink after all."

Relief gave him the strength he needed to crank the handle to wind the pail of water up. A full bucket would be heavier than an empty one of course; this one seemed ridiculously heavy - it took all his strength to push and pull the handle to wind up the rope and bring the bucket to the surface. Grimacing[35] with the effort of the final turn,

---

[35] grimacing – pulling a face because of the effort

Toby was flooded with relief as the slopping pail came into view. He reached over to take hold of the rope and swing the bucket over to himself to rest it on the wall of the well.

"You guys - will never believe - what is in - this - bucket!" Toby stammered, joyful disbelief crossing his face as he stared into the water that he was so keen to drink. He scooped up some of the sparkling water and tentatively tasted it from his hand. "Mmmmm…   that's d-licious!" he exclaimed. "It's so sparkly too…. Wonderfully sparkly…. Sur-pri-singly sparkly..." he drawled, trying to give clues to the other boys as to what was actually in the bucket. Inquisitively, they all peered into the bucket to see what was making Toby quite so delighted. They all cheered as they caught sight of the sparkling diamond – the fifth gem! It had been hidden in the bucket all along. Now they could move on to Level Three.

Before drinking any more water, Toby scooped some into his cupped hands and offered it to the little dog, who lapped it up greedily. All that crazy barking at goblins had made him particularly thirsty.

"Just as well you needed a drink, Toby!" exclaimed Bailey. "We'd have been searching high and low for that and never found it. I've never had a gem in the well before. We – and you – could have been stuck here forever!"

"Enough of that deep subject! Get it? A well…. Deep…. Stuck here forever… Get it?" laughed Biscuit. They all groaned – the normal response from the gamers for one of Biscuit's lame jokes.

"Let's get going!" urged Nick, "The timer has been going for fifteen seconds already while you've been joking around!"

They set off as fast as they could for the gate to Level Three, each carrying one of the gems and Toby carrying two. Scamp ran happily alongside Toby, glad to be part of the team. Arriving at the gate, they each placed their sparkling gems into a recess beside the gate; there was a place for each of the precious stones they carried. The first time they had placed all five gems the gate remained firmly shut. "Quick, we only have twenty seconds left – try other places. I'm sure the diamond goes on the top and the ruby below it," explained Bailey, the brains amongst them. "Try switching the others."

They tried another combination, but frustratingly the gate still didn't open. "Ten seconds guys…" Bailey continued, his eye on the clock. "You haven't tried the emerald at the bottom," he shouted, exasperated[36], "Quick, quick!" When all five spaces were finally filled with the correct gem, the blue gate swung open, revealing the urban landscape that was to be faced, and conquered, to achieve Level Three. Relieved, the four gamers dashed through, Scamp in Toby's arms – he was *not* going to be left behind!

---

[36] exasperated – frustrated that they were taking too long to get it right and time was quickly running out

7: TIM TO THE RESCUE

Meanwhile, back at Toby's house, his big brother Tim began to stir from a good night's sleep. As he gradually came to, he didn't realise where he was at first. He had just returned home after a trekking holiday in the Himalayas and had spent half the night on the computer, catching up with friends. He blinked rapidly several times to clear his vision, looked around his room at familiar things and sighed contentedly. It was always good to be home. The house was very quiet.

The bathroom was just along the hall, past Toby's room, where the door stood open, bed unmade, clothes strewn on the floor, exactly where they had been taken off. Tim raised an eyebrow in brotherly understanding. He'd not been the tidiest teenager himself. As he passed the door, he heard tinny voices coming from Toby's headphones, that were lying on the desk beside his PC. Toby must be downstairs getting something to eat… Tim quickly showered, ready for the day.

Padding back down the hall, he noticed that the same excited voices were coming through the headphones, but Toby was still nowhere to be seen. Taking the soft, carpeted stairs two at a time he went down to the kitchen to find him. Weird – there was no sight nor sound of Toby anywhere. 'How strange...' he thought. Selecting a cheerfully coloured mug, with extra-large capacity[37], he flicked on the kettle to make a cup of tea.

"I know what's missing!" he suddenly realised, muttering to himself: "Scamp." Could Toby have taken him for a walk and left

---

[37] extra-large capacity – one that could hold a lot of liquid

his computer in mid-flow? His forehead creased as he stared through his glasses into the distance of the leafy garden, trying to picture the scene. The bright flowers in the garden borders snapped into focus as he shook his head, grinning at the unlikely scenario of his brother voluntarily leaving his game to walk Scamp.

The violent bubbling of the boiling kettle brought him back to the present and the task of making tea. He poured the hot water onto the waiting tea bag and reached into the fridge for the milk. Maybe he'd have some cereal later, but first he wanted to go and find out what was going on with Toby's computer.

Climbing the stairs carefully, so as not to spill his tea on the new blue carpet, he started wondering what he would do with his day. He had looked forward to walking Scamp along the beach, but that would have to wait. Just across the landing, distant laughter and chattering still came from Toby's empty room, reminding him of his resolve to see why Toby wasn't playing computer games with his friends. Carefully placing his tea next to the keyboard, he nestled into Toby's large office-chair. Tim adjusted the headphones and began to listen to the conversation between the gamers.

As he clicked a random key, the screen lit up, revealing a game in progress: Escape! He peered at the screen to see which of Toby's friends were playing. He had joined in a couple of games last summer, so was vaguely familiar with the levels and the players Toby usually teamed up with: there would be Nick, Bailey, Harry, Biscuit and Ryan.

He watched, and listened, trying to work out where they were in the game. He was sure they were talking to Toby… but where was he? Tim watched as they placed their hard-earned precious gems into the correct nooks by the gate to Level Three, then dashed through the gate just before it slammed shut.

He could make out Nick, Bailey and Biscuit, since their nametags were floating above their avatar heads, but who or what was that other nameless character – and what on earth was that black blob jumping around beside him?

The more he pondered and listened, the stranger it became. They *were* talking to Toby

– was that him – the white and brown avatar? Why didn't he have a nametag, and why did he look a bit blurry and odd? "What?" he exclaimed, as he suddenly realised what he was looking at. He fumbled for the mic switch and blurted out, "Is that you Toby?"

8: LEVEL THREE - ALI BABA AND THE FORTY THIEVES

Toby stood, mouth-agape at the scene before him: seeing Level Three through a computer screen just gave a hint of the actual colour, size and wonder of the cityscape before him. Towering like an overgrown sunflower, the sky-scraping helter-skelter, that was the goal to be achieved in Level Three, sprouted from the centre of the irregular mass of buildings surrounding it: a haphazard[38] sea of colourful roofs, punctuated by sparkling, bejewelled domes and marble minarets.

---

[38] haphazard – no pattern or order to the way they looked

Narrow alleyways disappeared between the higgledy-piggledy buildings, snaking their way towards the central tower. The boys all knew the dangers lurking behind the shuttered windows and above, lying in wait on concealed balconies, under arches and market stalls, daggers drawn: Ali Baba's forty thieves, ready to pounce on unsuspecting gamers trying to reach the goal.

"Is that you, Toby?" coming from the sky, made Toby start. "Tim?" he asked, jaw dropped again in amazement as a familiar, but unexpected, avatar came bounding out from between two buildings.

"Are *you* a welcome sight!" exclaimed Nick, recognising Toby's brother from games played previously. "We were wondering how we were going to get Toby and Scamp ...."

"What!" shouted Tim, "You have Scamp there too?" At the sound of his voice, Scamp started jumping around and barking excitedly, somehow recognising this square-limbed, plastic avatar as Tim.

"Are you alright, boy?" Tim asked, bending down to pat his little friend. "Oh, how I wish I could scoop him up and give him a big hug."

"So, as I was saying," continued Nick, "we are a man down, so it was going to be tricky to get through this level. So, it's great you woke up in time to give us a hand."

"How did you get into the game Toby?" queried Tim. "No, don't worry – you can explain later. Let's just get you and Scamp back home safely, or Mum will.... Well let's not think about that. So, guys, what's the plan?"

"Well," explained Nick, taking charge,

"we were going to have Toby and Scamp in the middle of us and just go for it! But with four of us looking out for pesky thieves there's a much better chance of getting to the top of the helter-skelter."

The forty thieves from Ali Baba's sparkling city were the guardians of the towering helter-skelter and would use all their skills, and their sharp daggers, to prevent the boys from reaching the top. However, the boys would not face their quest unarmed.

Immediately after Nick had explained the plan to Tim, a great puff of golden glitter-smoke erupted in front of them… a laughing Ali Baba himself appeared, dressed in a bright red robe, pointy gold shoes and a dazzling white turban – just as if he had stepped out of a story book. His face broke into a gleaming smile as he handed Toby a key. This first key would get them through the door at the top of the helter-skelter – and to the slide they would whiz down to reach the final level – the watery Level Four.

"Guard this with your life," warned Ali Baba, staring intently into Toby's worried eyes, "or you will fail to escape." Words the boys

had all heard many times, but which had not had such a serious meaning before. Toby grasped the key and shoved it as far down as he could into his pocket. Toby would need to protect the key, but in turn, Biscuit, Nick and Bailey – and now Tim too – would protect him and his small, black, curly-haired companion. Toby looked around at the little gang around him: "I am so glad to be doing this with you guys – I wouldn't trust anyone else to get me out of here in one piece!"

Ali Baba carefully handed each of the gamers a lightweight, glinting scimitar[39] sword. They had beautiful jewel-encrusted guards, leather hilts and long curved blades, that shone almost as much as Ali Baba's even, white teeth. Scamp leant in against Toby's legs, a little afraid of this laughing, colourful character in front of them.

"Remember, you have just sixty seconds to get through the door at the top of the helter-skelter once you have eliminated all forty thieves. Anyone left on the wrong side of the door will not proceed to Level Four. So, run for your lives gamers and good luck!" With another puff of golden glitter, Ali Baba disappeared.

The lads prepared for the task ahead, swishing their flashing scimitars around like pirates, getting used to the weight and feel. To eliminate a thief, all they needed to do was to touch them with the tip of the scimitar, which sounded easy enough. The thieves, however,

---

[39] scimitar – a curved sword; pronounced 'simmitar'

were both agile[40] and cunning - avoiding their daggers was tricky enough without having to strike them back - and protect Toby too.

Toby was the key-bearer, so he had no scimitar, and had to rely on the skill of his team to get him safely to the top of the slide – with Scamp. Tim joining them was such a relief – greatly increasing their chances of success.

"OK team! Let's go!" yelled Nick, brandishing his scimitar and diving into the nearest alley. The others kept close behind, with Toby and Scamp sandwiched between them. Tim, at the back, faced backwards as much as he could, to watch for any thieves attacking from behind. As the alley narrowed, they slowed down and edged along, darting glances in all directions.

Biscuit gestured upwards, ahead, "Careful of that balcony," he whispered, indicating the ornate wooden balustrade built

---

[40] agile – able to move quickly and easily

out above the alleyway. The words had hardly left his lips when, from the shadows, leapt a screaming, turbaned thief, his dagger lunging at Nick, who was leading the band of gamers.

Quick as a flash, Biscuit thrust his sword up at the flying thief; immediately the sword's tip had touched his body, the thief dropped like a stone, landing in a lifeless heap beside them. The startled boys jumped in surprise and Scamp began barking and madly jumping around. Toby picked him up to calm him down and the boys cautiously continued on their way.

With a shriek, another thief launched himself from the shadows of a doorway. Quickly jumping aside and jabbing at the attacker, Tim left a second thief in a tangled heap on the path as his scimitar found its mark. The boys came to a small marketplace with alleys leading off in all directions.

Looking around, they wondered which alley to take to give them the straightest route to the centre of the marble city. Suddenly,

Scamp began barking and trying to wriggle out of Toby's arms…. Once on the ground, he crouched, growling at a covered market stall, teeth bared, ears pricked. Bailey stood ready to strike as Toby silently slid beside the stall. On Bailey's nod, Toby whipped up the cloth hanging over it. With a lunge and a quick jab of his sword, Bailey left thief number three immobilised.

"Well done Scamp!" grinned Toby, "You saved us there!"

"Let's take this path," decided Nick, pointing towards the largest of the three alleys, that seemed to lead off vaguely towards the helter-skelter.

As they dashed along the narrow passages between the marble buildings, more thieves attacked from all directions; each time, one of the boys managed to get their bejewelled[41] scimitar in the way, just in time.

The helter-skelter was getting nearer and

---

[41] Bejewelled – decorated with sparkling jewels

nearer – surely the red-brick archway at its base would be around the next corner? Once you were on the stairs in the game, it was easy to kill off the attacking thieves, so it was best to arrive there as soon as possible.

"Aaargh!" came a screech from an incoming thief, long black hair flying as he

leapt from a window ledge, right next to Bailey, and pounced on him. But he was left to deal with him alone…. at that instant, shrieking, dagger-wielding thieves came flying in from every direction, all attacking at once. Scimitars and daggers flashed and swished, jabbing and slicing as the boys fought bravely to protect the key-bearer - and the little dog. As one thief collapsed, lifeless, on the path, another was there to take his place.

Toby crouched in the middle of the battle, trying to shield himself behind his fighting friends. He desperately attempted to keep hold of Scamp, who was wriggling in fright at the din going on around him. "No!" he cried, as Scamp broke free and tore down a dark alley to escape the mayhem. Knowing he was taking a great risk, Toby dashed off behind the fleeing black shadow of his little friend.

The noise of the fighting faded as he tore down the alley. Soon, the only sound was the pattering of his own footsteps on the flagstone pathway, flying along as he tried to keep Scamp in his sights. Just as he turned the next corner, he glimpsed Scamp turning right, under a red-brick archway and bounding up the circular stairway in front of him. Quite by chance, he had discovered the entrance to the helter-skelter!

Toby dashed up the steps behind Scamp. He smiled with relief, slowing as he realised the little dog would have to stop soon: the heavy wooden door at the head of the winding staircase was locked... and he was the one who had the key. Arriving at the top, both he and Scamp sat panting, trying to catch their breath after the frantic dash up one hundred spiral steps.

"Sorry old pal – no water up here – but there's plenty where we are off to next, so don't worry," laughed Toby, relieved to have got through Level Three with both the key and Scamp. He wondered how long it would be before he was joined by his friends. Confident that they had the skills to kill all forty thieves and then get safely to the top of the helter-skelter, where he now sat, he knew it wouldn't be long.

In case they came pelting up the stairs with seconds to spare, Toby unlocked the door, prepared for a quick departure and descent to Level Four.

"Yeah! That was the last one, lads," Biscuit yelled as a fortieth thief lay inert on the flagstone pathway.

"We're not at the helter-skelter yet though," pointed out Tim, "we've only got sixty seconds…. well, less now…. to find the entrance and get to the top."

"So, come on then!" urged Nick, setting off in the right general direction. "Bailey, you clock-watcher, you keep counting us down to keep us going."

"Well, we're down to thirty-five, so run lads!" laughed Bailey.

"Down here…" indicated[42] Biscuit, "I can see the archway. Time Bailey?"

"Twenty. Just a hundred steps between us and a long slide down to Level Four!" Bailey chuckled.

Toby jumped to his feet as excited voices and laughter, could be heard in the distance, rapidly approaching as the boys ran as fast as they could along the alley to the

---

[42] indicated – pointing the way to go

helter-skelter. This was followed by the sound of plastic feet, clattering[43] frantically up the stairs. Toby picked up Scamp and stepped through the door, knowing that the speed at which his friends were running up the stairs meant just one thing… the clock was ticking - and sixty seconds was almost up. Just as he thought, the boys came flying up the final steps, launching themselves towards the open door.

"Quick! Quick!" urged Biscuit, pushing Nick and Bailey through the door. Tim was the last one up, flinging his body through the door; it slammed shut behind him as time ran out.

"That was fun!" whooped Nick. "That was so close... I thought we weren't going to make it!" There was much laughter; Scamp recognised the mood of the boys and started barking excitedly. The boys slid their scimitars into a box beside the door – *they* would not be any more use to them now. All the gamers

---

[43] clattering – making a loud noise

were relieved to get their avatars to the top of the slide that would take them into the final level of Escape! All that lay between them and their final goal was just a raging river - and the minor problem of the ugly river monster guarding the key – no sweat.

9 LEVEL FOUR – THE RAGING RIVER

Toby grabbed hold of Scamp, sitting him on his lap as he jumped onto a sack to slide down the helter-skelter. They set off like

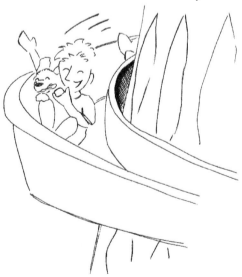

a rocket: hair flying, Scamp's ears pinned back, eyes gleaming in excitement.

"Yeahhh!!" Shouted Toby as they flew round and round down the slippery slide and under the archway into Level Four. They shot off the end of the slide and landed in a huddle together, laughing and barking. Toby rolled them out of the way as the others came piling through, whooping in excited laughter at the speedy descent from the tall, sparkling-marble tower in Level Three.

They sat up and gazed around them at the open, green hillside they were on and the raging white-water torrent[44] below – the river they needed to cross to get out of Escape! The bobbing, blue rowing boat, moored[45] the other side of the river, would carry them all, hopefully, to freedom.

Nearby, was a bright yellow well; another refreshment token to replenish[46] their

---

[44] torrent – a strong, fast-moving stream of water
[45] moored – tied up securely to the bank
[46] replenish – to fill up again

energy after all that fighting, was just what they all needed. Toby dug his hand in his pocket; with a smile of satisfaction, he pulled out a wrapped sweet. With all the action in the marble city he hadn't noticed his hunger, but now they had stopped, he realised he had come out without any breakfast – so the sweet he found was very welcome – his favourite sort of refreshment token.

"Are you ready for the last challenge, Nick?" asked Biscuit, staring at the water flowing fast in the valley below them, "Crossing the raging river!" Nick had the uncanny[47] knack of knowing exactly where the submerged stepping-stones were. As you stepped on one emerging stone, the next would suddenly rise above the level of the river – but only briefly. If you hesitated, or turned the wrong direction, you would not survive; more than once they had all been swept down the river and lost their lives – frustratingly close to the goal.

---

[47] uncanny – strange and mysterious

Nick was the expert, rarely falling into the raging torrent around him. He would then untie the boat and row over to pick them up.

"Yep," nodded Nick, striding purposefully towards the river. The starting point was indicated by a red mat on the near bank, almost opposite the boat.

Nick began the crossing, leaping just as the first stone broke the surface of the water and thankfully landing securely on it. He

immediately turned a little towards the left and launched himself, just the right distance, to land squarely on the next rising stone. Before it sank down again, he stepped neatly to the right, onto the next one. The boys shouted encouragement as Nick nimbly jumped from one stone to the next. He continued almost the entire width of the river... almost.

"No!" groaned the boys, leaping to their feet in dismay[48] as they watched their friend slip off the final stone and disappear beneath the water swirling around him.

"Yeah!" they cheered, as they saw him pull himself out of the water on the far side of the river. They knew he could do it.

"Well done Nick – saved us again!" cheered the gamers. However, it was only the first challenge of Level Four. Now the whole team would be needed to secure their exit from Escape! and return Toby and Scamp back to the real world.

Nick turned his attention to untying the little blue boat. Having jumped nimbly in, he sat down on the middle bench, shipped the oars and set off rowing across the raging river.

---

[48] dismay – a worried, sad feeling

He steered upstream a little since the current was pulling him downstream. He pulled steadily on the oars with all his might, and the boat made steady progress through the fast-flowing water.

As he neared the bank, the other boys grabbed the rope attached to the prow, bringing the craft alongside the riverbank. They all leapt in, apart from Scamp, who looked decidedly unsure about this unusual form of transport and refused to budge. Toby grumbled as he had to clamber back out of the boat, grab Scamp tightly, then carefully step back in. He kept tight hold of Scamp's collar as Bailey and Biscuit now rowed them all back across the river. Safely on the far bank, with the boat once again tied securely to the post, the boys considered their next move.

10: THE RIVER MONSTER AND THE KEY

They couldn't escape until they had gained The Key - the key to the door – the little door that had started this adventure and would also end it. The Key was hidden in a cave behind the waterfall that joined the river a little higher up. It was guarded by the river monster, which had claws like daggers, teeth as sharp and long as ancient stalactites[49] and a slashing tail that could whip around and knock you off your feet. Its mean, red eyes could be clearly seen following their every move from

---

[49] stalactites – a long, pointed piece of rock hanging down from the roof of a cave

behind the wall of water, noisily cascading[50] down in front of the cave.

"Tell me again how we are supposed to get past this creature?" asked Biscuit, hesitantly. "It's a while since I played Escape! to this level – I usually get killed off by goblins! Don't we get weapons?"

Nick chuckled, "No, Biscuit – we just go in and defeat him with our bare hands…. Of course we have weapons! The trick is hooking them out of the pool here below the waterfall. Can you see the daggers glinting down there? The water's deep but it's clear. Leaning against that tree," he explained, pointing to a leafy willow behind them, "are fishing rods with magnets attached, which we use to hook out our weapons. However, the longer it takes us to hook them, the shorter the blades get."

"Let's get going then!" exclaimed Toby, spinning round and striding to the tree. The others quickly followed, and all grabbed a

---

[50] cascading – flowing downwards

magnet rod. Taking up positions around the
pool, they began casting their lines into the
deep, clear water. Toby tried to lower the
magnet onto a silver blade, but it was a lot
trickier than it appeared to get it to land in the
right place. The other lads kept casting and
casting, until Tim let out a cry of success,

deftly[51] pulling up his magnet with a glinting,
long-bladed dagger attached.

"Yeah!" he exclaimed, triumphantly[52], as

---

[51] deftly – skilfully, cleverly and quickly, neatly
[52] triumphantly – very happy about his success

he closely examined the weapon which was going to help get his brother and dog back home. "Come on lads…. You can do it!" he encouraged, as the other lads continued to cast their lines into the clear pool.

At last, Bailey and Biscuit also managed to hook a dagger each, but with much shorter blades than Tim's. Nick and Toby finally each hooked a dagger too, but the blades were so short the boys just fell about laughing: their daggers just looked ridiculous and would be no use for fighting the river monster.

"Well three daggers will just have to do," decided Nick, "Toby, you just stand well back until we get the key – you have to survive even if all of us don't." Toby reluctantly nodded in agreement. He loved to be in the thick of the fighting, but this time there was too much at stake. It was decided that Nick would also stay out of the fight since he was the best rower: he would be essential to steer Toby and Scamp safely and speedily in the boat down the river, through the rapids, before time ran out.

"Remember," Nick reminded them, "we only have sixty seconds to ride the rapids and get to the finishing post across the lake once the key has been removed from the box. We don't want to sink so close to home. So, no hanging around – straight to the boat. Bailey, you sit in the bows, ready to hit the finishing button when we land, Tim you can help me row once we get through the rapids. Biscuit balance us out, sit in the stern and cheer us on. Toby, keep tight hold of Scamp – we don't want to lose him at this stage in the game!" Nick always led from the front, giving clear instructions, hating indecision. "But first, we will enjoy watching you guys slay the monster," he laughed.

As Tim, Bailey and Biscuit moved towards the waterfall, tightly gripping their daggers, the ugly red eyes of the river monster first followed their progress, then ominously disappeared. With a yell for courage, the boys charged behind the sheet of water – all that could be seen was the flashing of blades and the flailing, clawed, monster limbs. His teeth were long, like a walrus, and covered in slimy, yellow drool, which sprayed the fighting boys as he tossed his scaly, orange head. Each time a dagger found its mark, the monster roared and clawed at the boys.

Catching him unawares, the monster flicked his tail and knocked Biscuit off-balance; seeing the avatar fall to his knees, the screaming monster lashed out with a scaly claw and mortally wounded the brave gamer. Biscuit dropped his dagger, slumping slowly to the ground as his avatar turned red - his game-life ebbing away.

Realising they had lost their teammate,

Tim and Bailey fought with increased desperation[53] and determination, each time avoiding the sweeping tail of the orange beast – they *had* to kill the monster and get the key. Noticing that the monster was tiring, Nick started cheering when he saw the scaly beast was himself turning red. "Don't give up lads! You've wounded him – he's dying!" he yelled. This welcome news spurred on the two boys as they jabbed at the snarling monster with renewed vigour.

All the time, Toby had been closely watching how the monster reacted to the boys' attack. Down here on ground level, Toby could clearly see the monster's eyes; he realised the orange beast had very poor eyesight. Now was the time to suggest some daring tactics: "Tim, when you move very slowly the monster can't see you. You distract him, Bailey, with lots of jumping and shouting so that Tim can creep right up to him and get him in the heart with his long blade." Tim looked at him uncertainly. If Toby was incorrect, it was a

---

[53] desperation – feeling the situation is looking hopeless

certain death for Tim's avatar.

"OK. If you think it might work, it's worth a chance," Tim agreed. "Ready Bailey?" He nodded and leapt to the left, towards the tail end of the monster, jumping and shouting, wildly waving his dagger around in big, sweeping motions. The monster turned his great scaly head towards the commotion, his red eyes fixed on this bouncing green menace.

Sure enough, as Toby had predicted, with the monster distracted Tim was able to slowly creep right up to it. With a final, desperate surge of energy, he thrust his dagger right into the ugly beast's heart. Yellow drool rained down as the orange beast shook its head with a last angry roar of defeat; his body turned as red as his eyes. The two boys leapt swiftly out of the way as their nemesis collapsed in a scaly heap, onto the rocky floor of his lair. Dead.

With a cheer, Toby dashed into the cave. "Well done lads – that was brilliant!" he exclaimed, grinning. Excitedly, he slapped

Tim and Bailey on the back. "Shame about Biscuit, but he can come back and fight another day. Now it's time to ride the rapids – I'm ready for my lunch!"

Dodging past the tired fighters, Toby reached into the nook and grabbed the prize: the golden key, that was hanging in a nook in the wall, setting the final sixty seconds in motion.

11: THE FINAL CHALLENGE

Clutching the key, Toby scooped up Scamp and clambered into the waiting boat, quickly joined by the remaining three boys. Nick lifted the paddle and sat facing downstream, ready to adjust the direction the boat was facing if the rapids knocked it off course.

As the strong current caught the boat, they quickly picked up speed – the boys whooped with delight as the rapids tossed

them right and left. Even Scamp seemed to be
enjoying the ride, his eyes glinting in a nervous
way, but happy to be safe in Toby's arms. As
Nick deftly steered them around the jagged
rocks that peeked out above the surface of the
raging river, spray was flying around them,

thankfully washing off the smelly, yellow
monster-spittle that had stuck to Tim and
Bailey during the battle.

After a few brief moments of
exhilarating rapid racing, the little blue boat
slowed as the channel widened and the current
lessened. Trees now lined the river, that lazily

meandered[54] across the valley floor, but with the final clock ticking, there was no time to enjoy the scenery. "We still have thirty seconds, but Tim I need your strength to pull on the oars with me." Tim quickly took an oar and Nick turned to face the stern with him. Together they rowed in time, the little boat making a bow wave as it cut rapidly through the water.

Ahead, Toby noticed the sparkling lake – the lake where their fun adventure must end. A mixture of emotions hit him as he sat, clutching his little furry friend: relief, sadness and contentment all did battle within him. What an amazing adventure they had had – he almost wished he could do it all again; but now it was time to return Scamp to the real world – to step back through the little door. The light glinted off the golden key that Toby still held tightly, while the bump of the boat, as it gently came to a stop, brought him out of his thoughts.

---

[54] meandered – curved, bendy like a snake

"Quick Bailey," yelled Nick. "Clock's on 57.... 58...." Bailey, who had been waiting for this moment, leapt out as they touched the bank, hitting the button on the finishing post just before the sixty seconds was up.

"Phew, that was close again" exclaimed Toby, "But we made it! Well done team – brilliant effort. Thanks." Scamp, at least, was certain which way *he* was going. With a bark of relief, he followed Bailey and bounded out of the boat onto dry land, looking round with his warm, brown eyes at Toby, urging him to follow.

The friends clambered out of the boat and strolled towards the clearing in the trees where Toby had first met them, earlier that day. Was it really the same morning? A lot had happened in a short time.

Now that all danger was passed, and knowing that Scamp was safe, Toby took time to gaze around, trying to imprint on his memory the scenery in the game. "Time to go home, Toby," said Tim quietly, understanding

why his brother was almost dragging his feet as
he set off along the overgrown path that led
back to the door. Toby smiled ruefully as he
looked behind him at Tim, grateful for the
words that broke the spell.

The path was getting darker as they
neared the door, but there was just enough
light to see the trails of ivy either side of it, and
the keyhole that had been the first clue to his
location. He shook his head to rid himself of
the memory of that awful feeling earlier that
day of being alone – of being shut in – no way
to escape.

The key slid easily into the keyhole, turning with a welcome clunk as the snib withdrew, releasing the door. As Toby pulled it open, Scamp shot through the little doorway, worried that he would be left behind. Looking around, Toby just caught sight of the avatars as they exploded in a sparkling puff of plastic smoke – they would have to log in again if they wanted to start another adventure.

He smiled as he ducked back through the little door, wondering who would be the next of his friends needing to escape. His smile grew to a grin.... What a great summer *this* was going to be!

THE END

THE CHILDREN OF BURKINA FASO, WEST AFRICA

Burkina Faso, a small country in the heart of West Africa, just south of the great African Sahara Desert, is home to around 20 million people. Stepping off the plane at Ouagadougou, the capital city, was just like stepping through a 'little door' into a whole new world: colourful, bustling, noisy streets with bikes and motorbikes tearing around; many different languages being spoken; ladies carrying big silver bowls full of water, grain or who-knows-what on their heads; children walking with no shoes on their tough feet; and the heat… so hot.

Until the early 2000s, it was a peaceful country: education was developing quickly, with many new primary and secondary schools being built, along with transport links and sanitation. But then came the terrorists, across the northern and eastern borders. Many people had to flee their homes, leading to nearly 1 million people being displaced (having to live in another, safer part of the country) with no permanent housing and often struggling to find enough food to feed their families.

Some families have sent their children to safer towns to try and continue their education. Schools have had to take on many new students in already crowded classrooms; the government has found empty sheds and buildings to start new schools with displaced teachers running them. Often these children are without adult supervision, living in UN tents around the towns. This is not an easy way to gain an education, but children are desperate to learn - to get their qualifications – to escape poverty.

Thirty percent of the royalties from this book will be going towards helping children in Burkina Faso with their education. This may be to help pay the fees needed to attend secondary school, or to buy a uniform, or stationery, or equipment for living away from home. Thank you for your part in that.

Rachel and her family lived in Burkina Faso for fourteen years, in a house in 'the bush' (the African countryside). A hot and dusty place, their village was called Legmoin - seven sweaty hours' drive from Ouagadougou. She home-schooled her children, who loved to play outside with their Dagari friends, climbing trees to pick the fruit, catapulting rocks at cans, hunting for tarantulas – life was one big adventure. Two of her children loved to read – they devoured books – but one did not. I would like to think that this little story would have appealed to his sense of adventure and helped spark an interest in story books, which can open little doors into so many adventures of the imagination.

ABOUT THE AUTHOR

Rachel Nash is a teaching assistant in Dorset, where she lives with her family. This is her first novel. The story grew from a picture in The Mysteries of Harris Burdick, used in her Year 6 class for creative writing lessons. A group of challenged writers in a small group, together came up with the intriguing idea of a computer game being behind the little door in a cellar, that was the subject of one of the pictures. The idea developed over the next couple of years, inspired by her sons' online-gaming community of friends. She is not planning on giving up her day job but enjoyed the experience of writing and then publishing. She hopes the theme of the book will entice reluctant young readers to want to pick up a book – to catch the magic that reading can bring.

Like Rachel's children, Amelia Gibson, who illustrated this little story, also grew up in Burkina Faso. She is now living in the UK and building a career to use her delightful artistic talents.

Printed in Great Britain
by Amazon